alien expedition

BOOK #3 OF THE
[alien agent
series]

pamela f. service
illustrated by mike gorman

Carolrhoda Books · Minneapolis · New York

Carolrhoda Books
A division of Lerner Publishing Group, Inc.
241 First Avenue North
Minneapolis, MN 55401 U.S.A.

Website address: www.lernerbooks.com

Library of Congress Cataloging-in-Publication Data

Service, Pamela F.
     Alien expedition / by Pamela F. Service ; illustrated by Mike Gorman.
        p.   cm. — (Alien agent)
     Summary: Young alien agent Zack joins an archaeological dig in Mongolia to ensure that there is no trouble from the dinosaur-like scientists from Vraj's home planet who are on a similar dig nearby.
     ISBN: 978-0-8225-8870-2 (trade hard cover : alk. paper)
     [1. Extraterrestrial beings—Fiction. 2. Archaeological expeditions—Fiction. 3. Kidnapping—Fiction. 4. Mongolia—Fiction. 5. Science fiction. 6. Humorous stories.] I. Gorman, Mike, ill. II. Title. III. Series.
     PZ7.S4885Ali 2009
     [Fic]—dc22   2008020679

Manufactured in the United States of America
2 – S B – 4 / 3 0 / 1 0

[aLien agent] series

Prologue

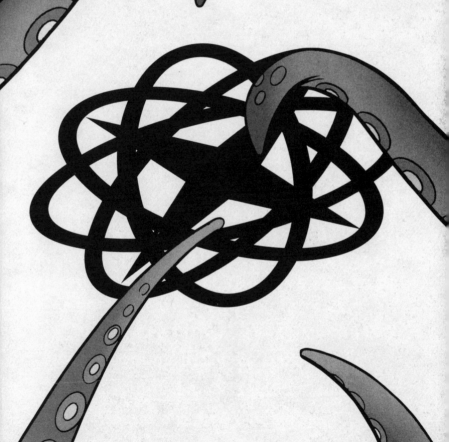

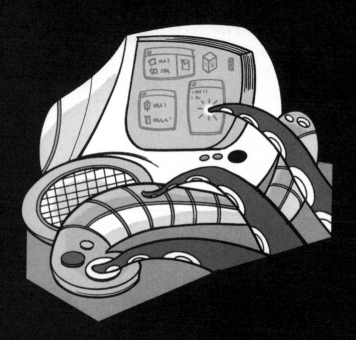

"I'm transmitting all the information you need for this job," Chief Agent Zythis said through the ship's communication screen. Agent Sorn watched as several of her boss's tentacles jabbed controls.

"The Galactic Union is counting on you, Agent Sorn," Zythis said. A half-dozen of his twelve eyes sparkled with confidence. Sorn tried to smile back as she closed the link.

Turning away, she glowered out her ship's view port at the stars flowing by through transluminal space. Usually, the colored streaks soothed her. Not now.

Annoyance sizzled through her. Here she'd been on an important mission to planet Quafeer Nine. Zythis's orders had just diverted her to an even more important mission on planet Earth.

When was the Galactic Union ever going to get enough personnel to handle this sector?

She particularly hated going to Earth. Oh, it was a nice enough place, even though it was not part of the Union yet nor even aware that other planets were inhabited. But Zack Gaither, the Union's planted agent there, was still too young and too untrained. He was being asked, yet again, to go on a possibly dangerous mission.

And *she* had to do the asking. Again.

Angrily she stalked to her makeup cabinet. With this new assignment coming when she was already in space, she hadn't been able to use the Union's Physical Transformation Service. Good thing her species was basically shaped like Earth humans. Her natural white hair would fit in. But not her purple skin. Pawing through bottles, she found a lotion that might do. It should temporarily turn her a light tan.

Frowning, she thought about the ship's wardrobe. Designed for Quafeer Nine, it was pretty flamboyant stuff. Still, she ought to be able to alter something.

Again, she cursed everyone involved in this situation. She had not gone through years of agent training to become a seamstress!

Grabbing a pair of sonic scissors, she went after her wardrobe.

CHAPTER ONE

"Hello, Zack," a voice said. I turned on the sidewalk and looked at the woman standing in the shade of a tree outside the school yard. My stomach tightened with fear and excitement. Despite her human-tinted skin and normal clothes, I recognized her. Agent Sorn.

It was a few weeks before summer vacation when I saw her waiting for me outside the school yard. She might have been someone's grandmother, a basically human-looking person with a shock of white hair. But the sight of her suddenly pumped me with adrenaline. After all, the two times I'd had anything to do with her before, I'd had plenty of excitement.

The alien lady smiled apologetically. "You probably hoped you wouldn't be seeing me again for a long time."

I smiled back. She might have been right a few months ago, but not now. After last summer's adventures, I thought I'd had enough of being a secret alien agent. Back then I was just looking forward to an ordinary school year as an ordinary human student.

But I guess the dangers and excitement had kind of seeped into my blood. I mean, over one summer I'd discovered I'm really an alien, adopted by unsuspecting human parents. I ended up working with good aliens and being chased and almost killed by bad ones. That sort of thing is kind of a rush—if you survive. So after a few months, ordinary school life had started to look pretty dull.

Still, I was resigned to it. I was looking forward to hanging out with friends this summer. However, my plans—once again—tanked. It turned out that Ken's family was going to Hawaii (tough life), and Jessica had to help her grandparents move to Florida. The summer was starting to look like a real bust.

Until Alien Agent Sorn showed up, that is.

After a slightly awkward handshake, we walked to the burger place near school. She said it was her treat, so I splurged on a root beer float and large fries, while she ordered a huge hot fudge sundae. "One of the plusses about visiting your planet," she whispered, as the waitress left with our orders. We'd chosen a pretty secluded booth. The kinds of things we were likely to talk about seemed to require spylike secrecy.

"How are you doing on the lessons that we're sending you?" she asked, as she plucked napkins from the dispenser. I guess she was familiar with messy sundaes. "Your parents haven't figured out that it's not regular e-mail?"

I looked around to see if anyone I knew was within sight. I could always explain away Sorn as a long lost aunt or something, but juggling too many lies gets complicated. "No," I whispered back, "and I'm careful they don't see me practicing. The self-defense stuff is cool, but learning how to use these powers of mine is kind of scary. I haven't got it all down yet."

"And you won't for a while. You're still too young. I wish I or some other agent could be here to teach you personally, but frankly our forces are way too thin in this sector. We just can't get to this planet very often. That's why it's so important to have you here, an agent who's been brought up as a human. You can act as an intermediary when the Galactic Union finally makes official contact with your planet. And, of course, it's good having someone on-site who can help out with little projects before then." We both smiled innocently at the waitress as she returned with our orders.

Sorn shoved a strand of white hair back from her forehead, gripped the spoon, and dove into her sundae. I took a slurp of my float and prompted her. "And you've got another little project for me now?"

Sighing, she said, "I really wish we didn't have to keep calling on you before you're older and fully trained, but something critical has come up on this planet. This new assignment should be easy, though. You probably won't have to do a thing besides enjoy a foreign vacation and be on hand just in case our other agent needs a bit of help."

"Sounds good," I said, dumping ketchup on my fries. "So where's this vacation?"

"Mongolia."

My hand jerked so much I sloshed ketchup on the Formica tabletop. She might as well have said Mars or Alpha Centauri or something. "You mean, like over by China?" I said as I hastily wiped up the ketchup with a wad of paper napkins.

"Between China and Russia. We've arranged for your parents to be invited to join an American expedition to the Gobi Desert this summer. And of course you'll go along. It's a real scientific expedition doing an archaeological survey. Your dad will soon learn he's the lucky, average, high-school science teacher 'randomly selected' to join the survey.

Of course, the real reason we arranged this is because the expedition is going to be in the part of the world where we need you."

"In Mongolia?" I said, picturing a lot of barren emptiness. "Kind of the ends of the Earth, isn't it?"

"It is rather remote from your point of view, I suppose. But it seems there's going to be another expedition there as well, unknown to anyone on this planet. It's from the Tirgizian Academy of Science. We tried to persuade them to hold off with their trip until the Galactic Union was ready to make contact officially with Earth. Unfortunately, the Tirgizians are not a patient people. And they have a lot of friends in high places, so their expedition is going ahead.

"They have sworn to keep their presence absolutely secret from the natives, but we thought it best to place an agent there to monitor things. And, as a backup to her, we need another agent who can work with humans in case anything goes wrong. That would be you."

"And your other agent can't work with humans?"

Agent Sorn smiled. "Well, she had a little trouble last year, I believe."

"Vraj?" I cried, and then lowered my voice, looking around to see if anyone noticed. At the other tables, no heads had swiveled our way. "Cadet Agent Vraj? Yeah, I'd say looking like a vicious dinosaur does make it kind of tough getting along with people. How come you chose her?"

"She's a Tirgizian herself. In fact her parents are part of the Tirgizian Academy of Science expedition. Apparently they were never very keen on their daughter becoming a Galactic Patrol cadet. But now it's proving useful to the scientists, because she can handle whatever contact is needed between them and the Earth-based agent—you. She is familiar with this planet, after all."

Vraj, I thought. She was a stuck-up, bossy, bad-tempered sort when we'd first met last summer—and still was at the end. But I'd kind of gotten to like her, in an odd sort of way. I'd even gotten used to my fellow agent looking like a velociraptor.

But this was no time for reminiscing. Not with all the questions bubbling in my brain. "So why is this bunch of scientists from a planet of dinosaurs on Earth anyway?"

"They're looking for their roots."

"Huh?"

"They have a theory that your Earth is their long lost planet of origin. Hundreds of millions of years ago, their ancestors were moved to Tirgizia, because the planet they lived on was about to be hit by a huge asteroid. A helpful galactic race, which has since disappeared, transported a sampling of the planet's dominant species to an uninhabited world to give them a chance to evolve. Those creatures did evolve. Tirgizians have become highly intelligent beings. They have long searched the galaxy for their mother planet. Their science academy expedition is hoping to prove that Earth is it."

"Well, I can see why you don't want them seen by the natives. Humans watch lots of movies about dinosaurs eating people and trampling cities."

"Exactly. But there's probably no danger. These are very cautious, responsible scientists, so Vraj's presence and your backup are just precautionary. And you get an exotic vacation out of the deal."

Scooping up the last smidgen of chocolate from of her bowl, Sorn reached for the bill the waitress had left, slightly smudged with ketchup and chocolate sauce. "At least I'm finally giving you an assignment where practically nothing can go wrong."

You'd think that I'd have learned by now not to buy that kind of line.

Several days later, I came home from school. My excited parents told me about the wonderful surprise trip to Mongolia they'd just learned about. Dad and our family had been "randomly" chosen to be part of this great expedition to the Gobi Desert. We would work on a survey of ancient human sites, while another part of the expedition would survey a nearby area for fossil remains.

It wasn't hard for me to act astonished. The idea of going to Mongolia was still boggling my mind. I mean, the place used to be called Outer Mongolia, and it was like saying "as close to nowhere as you could get."

It sure had that effect on my friends at school—definitely beating out Ken's trip to Hawaii or Jessica's Florida vacation when it came to the wow factor.

I started reading what I could about Mongolia in the library and online. Most things made it sound as wild as I'd imagined. One book was written by a guy who went there years ago, looking for dinosaur fossils. There were snakes, bandits, sandstorms, baking heat, and really bad roads. An ideal vacation spot all right.

But I was determined to do what Agent Sorn suggested. Offbeat or not, I'd treat this as pure vacation. Like she said, what could go wrong?

CHAPTER TWO

We spent a couple of weeks packing, repacking, and dealing with government paperwork. But a few days after school let out, my parents and I finally got on a plane for a long, long series of flights to the back of beyond.

I tried to act cool, as if I'd been on planes lots of times. But actually I hadn't. I suppose when I first came to this planet it was on a spaceship or something. But I must have been a really tiny baby because I don't remember any of that. At least I wasn't super nervous about flying the way Mom was. She kept saying how she really hated the hollow feeling of being thousands of feet up with nothing but air under us.

I decided to just sit back and enjoy this whole flying thing. I read the catalog from the seat pocket in front of me, selling lots of expensive stuff I didn't even want. I studied the plane's safety diagram, hoping that none of the stuff it showed would happen. And, of course, I stared out the thick little window.

My parents let me have the window seat. I couldn't get enough of watching the patch-work fields slip under us and the jagged tree-furred mountains with their snaking roads and hidden glints of lakes. And then there was the ocean—a whole lot of ocean. At first it was a huge, crinkly, blue sheet, and you could see waves and ships. Then we got too high to see anything but flatness. Even *I* finally got bored looking out the window, except when we glided through clouds piled up like gigantic, white mountains. There were in-flight movies and video games too, so boredom wasn't a problem.

The airline food was okay, but it got weirder and weirder as we changed to different national airlines. The little balls of raw fish and rice were particularly weird. I had to fight a desire to bounce them around the cabin. The airports got weirder and weirder too. The American airports were hurried and confusing enough, but the ones in Japan, China, and Mongolia could have been really bad. It was in them that I discovered the language implant that had been put in me last summer worked with Earth languages, as well as alien ones. I couldn't read the languages, but I could understand them and even speak them.

The problem was that my parents didn't know about any of this alien business. They thought they had adopted a regular human baby. So I couldn't let on that I knew what was being said in all these foreign languages. When airport staff tried speaking to us, their English wasn't exactly fluent. I pretended I kind of figured it out and nudged us in the right direction.

When we finally landed in Ulan Bator, Mongolia's capital, we were really tired. That whole trip had taken days. Someone met us at the airport and took us to a crummy little hotel. In the morning, things looked better. Not that Ulan Bator was much to look at when you think of capital cities like Paris or Tokyo. It was kind of a raw, sprawling place that seemed to be in the process of either being built or falling apart—probably some of both.

Still, we spent one day seeing the sights, including a museum with dinosaur fossils and eggs and mounted skeletons found years ago by that guy who wrote the book I'd read. We had lunch in the little snack bar, which was on a balcony overlooking the main dinosaur hall, and gazed down on the skeleton of a dinosaur related to Tyrannosaurus rex. I liked that view best, looking *down* on the guy. Earlier, when we'd been below and looked up into his teeth and claws, I started getting nervous about my assignment. I wasn't worried about working with Vraj. She was more or less my size, but she was just a kid. I hoped I'd never have to meet her parents.

Anyway, the next day we and a bunch of other people piled into jeeps and headed south toward the Gobi Desert. About two miles out of town, the paved roads quit. For the next eight hours, we drove at breakneck speeds over chains of ruts and holes that braided across the grasslands. There weren't any road signs to guide us. Our drivers, though, laughed, sang to Mongolian rock music blaring from the CD players, and generally acted like they knew where they were going. The jeeps swayed, bucked, and rearranged everybody's bones. We had to stop several times for someone to barf, but thankfully it wasn't me. Twice we stopped and asked directions from guys herding horses. Once we stopped for a hitchhiking woman and baby, picking them up in the middle of nowhere and dropping them off in the same sort of place.

Sure, it was an adventure, but I've got to admit, I was glad when the land started to look more like a desert. I hoped it meant we were getting nearer to our Gobi Desert destination.

Finally, we reached the base of a sprawling mountain, where a cluster of big canvas tents made up the expedition's main camp.

We were welcomed by the director, Dr. Longford, and other staff members. Then we were taken to the cook tent and seated on folding chairs around rickety wooden tables. Along one side of the sloping canvas walls, big metal pots were burbling on gas-fired camp stoves. From these, a chubby Mongolian lady ladled out bowls of greasy stew that turned out to be chunks of goat meat and carrots. The meat was tough and took forever to chew.

Good thing I didn't know then that goat would be basically all we'd eat for weeks. I got even less fond of it that afternoon. We watched the cook pick out a goat from one of the local herds and slaughter it for our next few meals. I don't think it's a good idea to meet your meat.

After lunch, all the new arrivals picked out tent sites and set up their tents. Yellow, blue, and red tents sprouted like mushrooms over this dry, grassy valley at the base of a sheer, granite cliff. I set up my tent way at the outer edge of the tent cluster. For years, when we went camping, I'd had to share my parents' tent. Finally, for this trip, they'd bought me my own one-person tent. It was great. Among other things, I wouldn't have my dad snoring in my ear. It was always like camping with a bear.

That night, we met with the other expedition members, including the group whose main work was several miles away in another valley. They were looking for dinosaur fossils. The rock over there was sandstone, the type you find fossils in. My folks and I were with the group looking for archaeology stuff, remains of ancient human occupation—like Indiana Jones did.

The next day, the staff trained us in surveying. It was pretty simple really. Everybody stretches out in a long line, about thirty meters apart (that's about thirty yards) and walks forward, keeping their eyes on the ground.

Whenever anyone finds something like a scatter of broken pottery or chips from stone tool-making or maybe a bunch of stone slabs marking a grave, that person yells out "site!" Then everybody rushes over, takes pictures, records things in notebooks, and takes a GPS reading. It was kind of weird to think that here in the middle of nowhere, satellites were passing overhead that could locate you down to feet and inches. But I guess it's no weirder than knowing that hiding somewhere nearby were evolved dinosaur scientists from a distant planet looking for the same sort of thing that the paleontologists in the next valley were after.

The first day's surveying was fun, but it was really tiring. It was easy enough at first when we were covering flat ground where boots just crunched over gravel and skirted clumps of spear-sharp grass. But then my line ran into a rock outcrop. I looked around to check what the others were doing. Sure enough, they were keeping to their lines, maybe cursing a little, but going straight up. There were actually lots

of ledges and footholds in the rock. But after
pulling myself up and then scrambling down
the opposite sides for a while, my legs felt like
overcooked noodles. I was really glad I had
a compass. I could have gotten totally lost
among all the clefts and rock pinnacles. As the
hot day wore on, though, I did manage to find
a couple of sites, a scatter of potsherds (broken
bits of pots), and a Buddhist inscription on a
rock face. That was pretty exciting. At least I
could stop worrying that as the youngest team
member, I'd let the others down.

That first night, as we were settling down
to bowls of goat fried-rice in the cook tent,
Dr. Schultz, the head of the paleontology crew,
poked in his head. He said he wanted to report
some strange doings at their worksite. I was
so tired I could scarcely chew my goat chunks,
but a tiny warning bell went off in my head.
I forced myself to listen—though the electric generator that powered our one dangling
light bulb made a steady rumbling sound that
threatened to lull me to sleep.

"It looks like we've had a theft at our lab tent," he said, "so I wanted to warn you to keep your eyes open."

"What was stolen?" Dr. Longford asked, waving the other man to an empty seat.

Dr. Schultz joined us at the table but quickly declined the offer of goat and rice. "Several notebooks recording recent finds and one protoceratops egg." He frowned. "We'd already copied the notebooks, and that egg wasn't the best specimen. There were others in better condition in that nest. But it's disturbing."

Longford nodded his bald head. "Any clues? Footprints or anything?"

The fat paleontologist laughed. "Plenty of footprints, but that's what makes me think maybe somebody's playing a joke. They look like great big dinosaur footprints."

Longford laughed too, but I nearly choked on my goat. So much for the Tirgizians' pledge to be inconspicuous. Well, I reasoned, as long as no one saw them, it would probably be okay. But Vraj, wherever she was hiding, had better realize that her people, scientists or not, can't just walk off with stuff and not even bother to hide their tracks.

Annoyed, I kept chewing. I couldn't even tell her that unless she contacted me first. She definitely was not the sort to ask for help or advice unless she had to.

The next day, the survey really got into the rocks. Dragging myself up a cliff face, I was uneasy, remembering my reading about poisonous snakes and Gobi bears. Too many rocks were around for me to see any of my fellow surveyors. I was tempted to just sit a moment and admire the vast blue sky and puffy little white clouds. Mongolia is like those places in the American West, like the Big Sky Country. But I didn't want anyone to have to look for me. And I didn't want them to think that because I was a kid, I couldn't keep up. So I forced myself to grab another ledge and pull myself up.

Just as I neared the top, a face snaked down to meet mine. A reptilian face. Lots of teeth.

"Vraj!" I gasped, clutching the ledge. "Don't scare me like that."

She sneered in her dinosaur-like way. "Yeah, happy to see you too." The same charming personality I remembered.

I crawled the rest of the way up. "So how come you let your scientists steal that stuff? They could have been seen and messed up everything."

"I didn't *let* them. Ever try to give orders to your parents? I told the Agency it was a dumb idea putting me, of all the people in the universe, in charge here. Parents and their coworkers are bound to treat you as a kid. Anyway, they took the egg, and now they are really excited about the DNA samples from it. They say it proves their theory. Frankly, I don't care what happened on this miserable planet millions of years ago. I just want off it now!"

I scowled, offended for my adopted planet. "Well, I'm sure we don't want your crew here much longer either. Just get them to put back the stuff they took, and then they can fly home with their great scientific discovery. End of assignment."

"Exactly my hope. I'm taking the notebook and the fossil back myself. The adults are so big and clumsy, they nearly blew it. Then you needn't worry about seeing me anymore." She gazed dejectedly over the barren landscape.

I felt a jab of guilt, remembering how Sorn had said that Vraj's parents had wanted her to become a scientist and not join the Galactic Patrol Corps. "Oh, yeah, well, I guess this hasn't been too warm a reunion. Sorry. How's it going in the Galactic Patrol Academy?"

She scratched her long, snaky neck. "Okay, I guess. The coursework is going fine. But I can't afford failing a field assignment, and this one is just ripe for that. Parents!"

"Yeah. Parents never really get it that kids grow up and have to live their own lives."

Twisting her tail tip in her clawed hands, she nodded. "So I guess this is hello and good-bye. Enjoy the rest of your rock-climbing vacation. And, by the way, your planet's not all that bad, really. I guess I don't mind having some ancestors from here. Distant ones, that is."

She slipped off among the rocks before I could even finish saying, "Thanks. And good luck."

When I caught up with the rest of the archaeologists, they were all excited over a stone wall about a foot high, some sort of winter animal corral, they thought. I was kind of down. Here was the end of the Alien Agent part of this adventure. That left me with weeks of looking for dead people's graffiti and broken pots and discovering how many ways there are to cook goat. Could be worse, I guess. I could be hanging out at home while my best friends were away on vacation. At least I can send them postcards from an exotic-sounding place.

In fact, things actually got better. The next morning, after reporting that our neighbors' fossil egg and notebooks had been mysteriously returned, Dr. Longford suggested that instead of surveying, I might want to spend some time with one of the local Mongolian boys. He said a boy named Jargul was about my age, and his family's herds and yurt were near our camp. The kid knew a little English from school and could maybe take me horseback riding.

That perked me up a lot. I'd read about Mongolian yurts, round tents that could be taken apart and moved along with their herds. And I love riding.

Jargul and his sister, Segi, showed up midmorning, riding brown horses and leading a tan one with a long black mane and tail. A really long tail that almost swept the ground. It seems Mongolians never cut them. Both kids wore shorts and T-shirts. Segi's long, black hair was held back in a ponytail with a pink plastic Little Mermaid bauble.

Their English was recognizable. They proudly told me that they went to school several months a year in a town near their family's winter camp. But because of the language implant, my Mongolian was a lot better than their English, so I told them I'd been studying for our trip and wanted to practice it.

Jamming a foot into the metal stirrup, I swung up into the small, high-backed wooden saddle. It wasn't quite as uncomfortable as it looked, but I couldn't see how really big guys could fit into them. The bridle and reins were mostly twisted rope, but the horse clearly knew what it was doing. Soon we were riding across the grassland. It was great. The gait was a little jarring, but at least Mongolian horses are short, almost like ponies, so it wasn't too far to the ground.

I managed to stay in the saddle and even helped them herd some of their goats toward a well. The horse did the herding, really, but we took turns hauling up water in a leather bucket and pouring it into a stone trough where the goats climbed over one another, getting drinks. Jargul and Segi taught me the various yelps, whistles, and calls that supposedly make the goats obey them. Still, obedience doesn't seem to be what goats do best. They're cute, curious creatures, and I regretted even more that they made up most of my diet.

We stopped for lunch at their grandmother's yurt. Jargul and Segi may wear ordinary Western clothes, but when their grandmother came to the door of the round white tent, she was dressed like the traditional Mongolians I'd seen in pictures.

She wore a long green robe belted at the waist and embroidered boots with upturned toes. After ducking inside the low, wooden door, I noticed the lattice sides and spokelike roof poles of the movable yurt. I could also see that the television was connected to a satellite dish and electric generator outside.

She switched off a cartoon program as soon as we stepped inside and gestured for us to sit on the colorful rugs spread over the floor. In the center of the yurt was a potbellied stove with a kettle of water heating on top. Granny creaked open the door of the stove and, taking the lid off a basket, tossed in some more fuel—kind of odd-looking fuel.

"What's that?" I whispered to Jargul.

He grinned. "Dried horse dung."

Don't look like a shocked foreigner, I told myself, but I'm not sure my face obeyed. Meanwhile, Granny had pulled big china bowls from a painted wooden cupboard. She ladled them full of goat yogurt and passed them to the three of us. I tried not to gag. Anyway, it tasted better once she dumped in a bunch of sugar.

As I ate the yogurt and fried dough balls, I studied my hostess. Granny was probably the wrinkliest person I'd ever seen, but her smile gleamed among the bronzed wrinkles. She hopped about as spry as a bird. At first I thought she was bald, and then I saw the gray stubble and realized that her head was shaved. Granny and the kids asked me lots of questions about life in America. They thought every-thing I said about my life or asked about theirs was very funny.

Then Granny went to her cupboard again and brought out a little orange silk bag. Squatting on the rug, she poured out the contents— knobby, whitish things. "Sheep knucklebones,"

Jargul whispered to me. "Granny wants to tell your fortune."

The old lady scooped up the bones, shook them in her hand, and muttered something I couldn't quite catch, even with my translator. She spilled them out on the rug again. For a moment, she studied their pattern, but she didn't say anything. Then she grabbed them up and spilled them out again. After repeating this several times, she abruptly scooped up the bones, dropped them in the bag, and sat back staring at me.

"Well?" I said after a moment.

After a longer silence, she shook her head. "Much strangeness, much danger." The look she gave seemed to shiver right through me. Then, slowly, she smiled. "Still, I am privileged to do your reading, foreigner Zack. Never have I seen one like it. Most in your reading, I do not fully understand. But there is rightness in you and in what you are doing, despite the dangers. I am comforted that my grandchildren accompany you."

That left me confused. Surely there wasn't much danger ahead now that the Alien Agent part of my stay was over. I frowned, wondering if she meant snakes and bears. Then she laughed and forced more yogurt on us until Jargul said we had better be off so we could round up the goats for milking.

It wasn't as easy as it sounded. Goats are very stubborn. But it least it kept my mind off knucklebones and weird fortune-telling.

When I was back at camp at the end of the day, washing up for yet another meal of goat, I decided that this really could be a good vacation, even if the only unfamiliar people I dealt with from now on were Mongolian goat herders.

I think I've mentioned how extremely wrong I can be about these things.

CHAPTER THREE

After dinner (goat on pasta), we archaeologists, experienced and amateur, worked in the lab tent, sorting potsherds. It was sort of like doing jigsaw puzzles, something my parents have always liked a lot better than I do. I told my folks about my day as a Mongolian goatherd, and they talked about their finds. Then after daylight gave out, we said good night and wandered back to our tents.

I sat outside mine, watching the orange sunset fade to purple then black. The nights in Mongolia are really amazing. The hot, desert day quickly changed into a chilly, desert night. I counted the first crop of shooting stars— there were so many. And the sky was so black.

There was no pollution or electric lights for miles, unless you count our one light bulb and Granny's TV.

Finally, I crawled into my tent and sleeping bag and lay there listening to the snuffling and chomping of a horse herd that was wandering through camp. The animals were all free range and seemed to think that every inch of grassland was their rightful pasture. I was just falling asleep when the peaceful horse sounds changed to whinnies and sudden galloping hoofs—like something had scared them.

It scared me too. Something was growling and scratching outside my tent. Then with a screech, the zipper door ripped open. Teeth glinted in the starlight.

"Vraj!" I quavered as my trembling flashlight lit her yellow-green face. "You've got to stop scaring me like that. . . . But, hey, I thought you'd be gone by now."

"I should be," she hissed. "But the others really *are* gone."

"So they left already. That's good."

"No, it's not! They're gone, as in disappeared. They haven't left the planet, their ship's still here. They've just vanished!"

"Vanished? Big dinosaurs? How many of them are there?"

"Eight scientists, including my parents."

"And they didn't leave you any message or anything?"

She snorted. "Would I be here if I had the least clue where they are? They'd set up camp in a shallow cave over in the next valley. All their equipment is there, but they aren't."

I frowned. "The next valley is where the human paleontologists are working. Maybe your group saw our group coming and hid."

"Ridiculous. Their cave had a conceal lock on it. They could hide there, and no one outside could find the entrance."

"Could they still be exploring?"

"No. I told you they were finished here and getting ready to go home."

Scrambling to pull on my jacket, I crawled out of the tent to join her. I was afraid the thin tent walls wouldn't hold if I asked her in. "Well, there's not a lot I can do besides help look for them tomorrow. Maybe it's time to contact the Galactic Patrol."

I think she rolled her eyes, but it was hard to tell in just the starlight. "I've done that! Or tried to. My communication channel is blocked. Like somebody's jamming it."

"Oh." Suddenly I felt a lot chillier. This assignment was taking a bad turn, and I didn't want to hear that Vraj and I might be on our own. "Well, there's probably some simple explanation for all of it, but I guess the best we can do is search the area. There should be some clues. I mean, these folks are kind of big, right?"

"Big enough to stomp you into dust, if need be. But yeah, search the area. Big help. That's all I was able to come up with too. Well, what did I expect? You've been on exactly two assignments, right? I'll be in touch."

What an annoying person, I thought as she slipped off into the darkness. But scared too.

I rushed into the night and called softly after her. My tent was fairly far from the others, but I didn't want anyone to peek out and see my visitor. "And keep trying your communication thing. I'll try to help you search tomorrow."

Without any e-mail here, I realized I didn't have any way of getting in touch with Sorn or anyone off planet. I really hoped there was some simple explanation for this turn of events—one that didn't put Vraj and me in charge of this planet's future.

The next morning, during a breakfast of millet and goat milk porridge, my parents talked excitedly about the kinds of pottery fragments they were finding. I had a sudden urge, quickly suppressed, to get up and hug them. They were here with me, enjoying their adventure, not vanished somewhere on an alien world like Vraj's parents. I had to help her find them—and not just because it was part of my assignment. She was a friend, in a prickly sort of way. And parents are important, even when they're pains.

It seemed there ought to be some way I could get Jargul and Segi to help me search, without telling them what we were searching for. I started piecing a plan together, but when they arrived on horses after breakfast, Granny was with them, and my feeble plan fell apart.

"Granny's inviting you to go with us to an *ovo* blessing," Jargul said proudly, after he and his sister got off their horses. Then he lowered his voice. "It's a great honor. She says you have a strongly spiritual aura about you. To her, you don't feel like an outsider at all."

Wouldn't she be surprised if she knew just how much an outsider I really was? I thought. "What's an ovo?"

Beside him, Segi giggled. "Spiritual, maybe, but you sure don't know much." She explained, "An ovo is a sacred mound of stones built up over years to honor the spirit of a place. Usually they're at mountain passes or peaks."

Jargul chimed in. "Granny's not just our grandmother. She's the one around here who knows the old ways and does what's needed to keep the gods and spirits happy. Come on."

All the while, Granny had been sitting on her horse, grinning encouragingly. I couldn't refuse, I realized. Well, maybe I could ask the spirits where the Tirgizians were. At least if we were heading for a mountain peak, there might be a good vantage point to search from.

When I popped back into the tent to ask my folks if I could go, they happily agreed. Parents are always pushovers for the idea that their kids are making new friends. And of course I was. They didn't have to know all the details.

As we trotted away from camp, I wondered which of the local mountains we were heading for. None of them were huge, but there were a lot nearby that looked like some giant had thrown down big wads of clay. Urging my horse up beside Segi's, I asked which mountain we were heading for. She pointed toward one, but when I asked its name, she giggled again.

"Silly, I can't tell you that! Never say a mountain's true name within sight of it, or its spirit will be offended."

Right. I sure couldn't afford to offend any spirits at the moment. I needed all the help I could get.

We followed a trail that cut through a steep, narrow valley and up onto a rocky plateau. From there, the actual peak of the mountain wasn't very far above us. Finally we dismounted, hobbled our horses, and started up a faint, rocky track. Granny scrambled on ahead, agile as a spider—a bow-legged spider. She must have been riding horses for eighty years.

I was a lot more out of breath than she was when we got to the top. It was windy up there. Sudden gusts blew hard enough to almost knock us off our feet. Segi was wearing a fleecy jacket over her pink T-shirt. Jargul wore a traditional-style blue-wool robe, though he had his shorts on underneath. It may be summer in a desert, but I was glad for my own hooded jacket. The gusting wind whipped at rags of blue cloth that fluttered like tattered flags from a gnarled stick. It was stuck into the top of a large pile of stones. Around the stones were smaller piles of skulls. Horses and goats, I thought.

Immediately Granny picked up a loose stone from the ground, placed it on the ovo, and began walking around it, clockwise. Jargul and Segi followed her, and with a shrug, I did the same. After three circles, Granny stopped, fussed around in the big bag slung over her shoulder, and pulled out a small rug. Spreading that on the ground, she sat down and then unwrapped a little bronze bowl filled with weedy-looking stuff. She fumbled with a cigarette lighter until the incense was lit and then began chanting prayers and running a long string of beads through her fingers. Jargul, Segi, and I sat on the rocky ground and watched.

The chanting, the incense, and the warm sun almost put me to sleep. What woke me up, though, was when Granny pulled a big white seashell from her bag and blew on it. She also jangled cymbals and beat on a little round drum.

All this seemed to go on for hours. Sometimes I tried to focus enough to look around at the crags and ravines dropping away from our peak. I didn't see any sign of missing dino-saurs, just endless rocky folds and towers of yellow, brown, and gray. I'd start getting antsy about all the time I was wasting, sitting there, but then the chanting and incense would wash over me again.

Finally Granny stood up and reached for the covered pot that Segi had carried up the mountain. She dipped in a ladle and began walking around the ovo again, splashing it with what looked and smelled like goat yogurt. *That* certainly broke the spell.

When Granny began packing up all her stuff again, Segi whispered to me, "We're finished now. The spirit of this place is content for an-other year. Granny's going home, but she said we might want to show you around for a while."

"Okay," I said, relieved I could now get on with my task here, hopeless as it seemed.

It wasn't long before Granny had scrambled down the rocky peak and rode off on her shaggy horse. Beside me, Jargul was pointing off into the distance.

"That's a dry lake bed over there. The ground's all white and crackled, and nothing much grows there. But over there ..."

Suddenly he grabbed my arm. "Look! I've been coming with Granny to make offerings to the spirits for years," he whispered. "But I've never actually *seen* a spirit before."

I followed where he pointed now. Partway down our mountain, on the other side from where we'd left the horses, was a dark figure. It was jumping about and waving in a frenzied, dinosaur-like way.

CHAPTER FOUR

My mouth went dry. "Oh. Yes. A spirit."

"What should we do?" Jargul whispered. "I wish Granny hadn't left."

"It seems to want us to come down," Segi said. "Should we? Spirits can be dangerous."

My mind raced. "Maybe I should go check it out first. I mean, since I'm not from around here, a local spirit shouldn't have any power over me."

"You're awfully brave," Segi said as I began climbing down. I felt like a fraud, but I wasn't afraid. I was angry. Why had Vraj shown herself?

When I finally reached her, the arrogant dinosaur was leaning casually against a rock.

"What do you mean doing that?" I blurted. "Those two humans saw you!"

She sneered. "I've been trying to get your attention for hours, but you were sitting there in a stupor. A lot of help you are, Agent Zack."

I tried to calm down. "Okay. Sorry. That was kind of a weird ceremony. But now what do . . ." I looked back up the slope and groaned. Jargul and Segi were climbing down toward us.

Turning back to Vraj, I snapped. "Hold on a minute. Those two think you're a spirit, a mountain spirit. They believe in those things." No less likely than dinosaurs from outer space, I thought, but I didn't say it. "So sit down on that rock and look spiritual. And anything you want to tell me, do it in a singsong chant."

She groaned, but sat and crossed her legs like a statue of Buddha. "You mean sound like that wizened old female did for hours? They didn't tell me there'd be this much indignity to being a Galactic Patrol Agent."

"Just do it," I growled as Jargul and Segi came closer.

She hissed back at me. "Well, I'll chant if I must, but I'll do it in Tirgizian. Maybe I can understand your painfully stupid Earth languages, but my throat refuses to speak them. Translate however you want."

The two stopped several yards away and lowered their eyes. "Granny was right, Zack," Segi said. "You *are* extraordinary. You can talk with spirits."

"A dragon spirit," Jargul breathed excitedly. "We are honored."

"Er . . . yes. And . . . and she has an important message for us so she's letting me understand spirit talk."

Vraj shot me a brief glower, then closed her eyes and began chanting Tirgizian in a high singsong voice. "Listen up, Zack. I got a message from my parents. They've all been kidnapped. A Kiapa Kapa Syndicate is holding them for ransom or something."

"Who are . . ." I began in Tirgizian, then stopped and chanted it. "What is a Kiapa Kapa Syndicate?"

"Interplanetary criminals! They're very powerful and even run some planets. The Galactic Patrol is always fighting some scheme of theirs and doesn't always win."

"So how did your parents contact you? Where are they?"

"If I knew where they were, I'd be trying to get them out now, wouldn't I? I got a brief message on my communicator—before it went blank again. I'll quote. 'Vraj, Kiapa Kapa holding us. Will try to learn and send location. Somewhere high. Get help.' That's all. The Kiapa Kapa must be messing with our communications. So you are all the 'help' there is here, worse luck."

A moment's spurt of anger sank under a wave of hopelessness. Then I turned and saw Jargul and Segi's wide-eyed gaze. "What is the spirit saying?" the girl whispered shyly.

"Ah, yes. She's saying that she needs help. You . . . eh, you know about good spirits and bad spirits?"

They both nodded solemnly.

"Well, some bad spirits have captured some other good spirits, and she needs to find and free them."

"And where are they?" Jargul asked.

"She doesn't know exactly. The bad spirits are very sneaky. Just that it's someplace high."

"High," Jargul repeated, looking out at the landscape around us, a landscape dotted with peaks and plateaus and rock pinnacles.

Vraj broke in, talking to me in singsong Tirgizian. "You really think these weak little natives can help?"

I chanted back, "Stow it. They know this area a lot better than either of us do. And your cover's okay as long as they think you're a dragon spirit. Can you breathe fire?"

She shot me a look that was as good as fire.

"Okay, never mind. Anyway, European dragons, I think, are supposed to breathe fire, not Asian ones. So just look wise and spiritual and in need of help."

I turned to Jargul and Segi, switching into Mongolian. "This is a very young spirit, she tells me. She came from afar to try to free her fellows and she doesn't know this area. Would you two be willing to help?"

Jargul bowed. "We would be honored. But why doesn't she also ask help from the other local spirits? The birds, animals, and rocks might know something."

Vraj, with her own implant, could understand the Mongolian as well. I heard her muttering in Tirgizian behind me. "Right, talk to the rocks. Great advice, that is."

Instantly I felt defensive and snapped. "Well, sure, rocks may be out, but the local birds and animals might have been disturbed by all you aliens tromping around. Maybe we could sense something from them."

It was a pretty feeble idea, I knew, and I expected Vraj to bite my head off, verbally anyway. But instead, she said thoughtfully, "These language implants do let us communicate with other species, as much as their intelligence allows. I suppose we could get the word out to some of the local creatures and find out if they know anything that might help."

So that is what we tried to do. The first challenge, of course, was the horses. When we walked around to the other side of the sacred peak, they totally freaked as Vraj approached. You could hardly blame them. You don't need to have seen a bunch of science-fiction movies to know that big, toothy dinosaurs are trouble. I'd never thought to try this language implant thing on animals. But then we don't have a lot of pets because of my mom's allergies. And anyway, I don't think goldfish would have much to say.

The horses were straining against their hobbles so wildly I thought they'd break their legs. Shooing Vraj back, I walked up to my horse and clamped my hands on both sides of its head. Isn't that what Mr. Spock does when he tries a mindmeld? I didn't have a clue what to do after that so I just thought, "Calm, calm, smooth and calm like water. Silly little lizard. Nothing to fear. Friendly lizard. Be calm. Horses stronger than lizards. Calm, powerful horses."

I don't know if I was getting through, but oddly enough, I did seem to feel bits of horse thought, stuff about running and grass. And the animals did become a little calmer.

I looked at Jargul and Segi, who were walking cautiously up to their horses. I tried to sound like I was on top of things. "Okay, I guess what we're going to do is . . . is ride along and . . . and whenever we see animals or birds or something stop and . . . try to talk to them or think to them and . . . and let them know we're looking for a bunch of big dragon spirits. They may know something."

I felt really lame saying this, and I could feel Vraj mentally chuckling at me. I turned to her and ordered in Tirgizian, "You. Just follow along and talk to whatever you see. But try not to spook anything."

"Yes, boss," she said sarcastically. A sarcastic dinosaur, even when it's pretending to chant, is not a pleasant thing.

First it was marmots—shuffling, brown things like big, furry slippers. We tried thinking down their marmot holes. Occasionally one would stick out its round head and give us a beady stare. Then there were hopping things that looked like long-legged mice with fur-tipped tails. A few stopped in their flight to stare back over their shoulders. I picked up a scattering of jittery thoughts, but I don't know if it was them or just me getting flipped out.

Jargul and Segi didn't have implants, of course, but they knew where to find animals. Who knows? Being locals, maybe their efforts were as good as mine or Vraj's. There were lots of birds too, and of course, plenty of goats, cows, horses, and sheep. I didn't get the impression that any of the creatures had seen large dinosaurs lately—other than Vraj. And she definitely did seem to make them twitchy.

We even tried the mental questioning thing on a bunch of camels. They'd been sheared of their wool and looked really odd with their two humps all naked and floppy.

Maybe it was my imagination, but their mental response seemed to match their sneering expressions. They couldn't care less about us or our problems. And they were bigger than Vraj, so she didn't seem to impress them either.

Finally Jargul and Segi said they had to return to their yurts but would meet me in the morning. Watching them ride off, I shook my head, unsure if we had really gotten through to anything. Vraj claimed that she had, but she could have just been boasting. All I could claim was that I'd gotten some really weird, flighty, skittery thoughts bouncing back into my head.

When I told Vraj I didn't think this was helping much, she got snotty and stomped off into the growing dark, snarling, "Why should you care anyway? It's not *your* parents or *your* career as a Cadet that's at stake."

"Well, yeah, but it is *my* assignment," I called back. "And I want this to work. I just don't know if this talk-to-the-animals thing is getting us anywhere."

"If you come up with a better idea, native boy, tell me in the morning. I'll be here early."

Annoyed and discouraged, I tromped back to the cook tent. The archaeologists and paleontologists were buzzing about their finds of the day. They had discovered some Turkic inscriptions and a new deposit of dinosaur fossils.

I tried to look enthusiastic, but I really didn't care much. My mind wasn't on fossil dinosaurs but on live ones. Dinosaurs who'd managed to get themselves kidnapped and were depending on a couple of clueless, inexperienced Alien Agents to free them.

Their eyes glowing with their exciting finds, my parents didn't notice the cloud of gloom over my head. "I'm really glad you're having fun with your young friends," Mom said, over our bowls of creamed goat. "But don't forget tomorrow is Saturday, so it's only a half work day. They're planning on having some traditional Mongolian wrestling in the afternoon. You don't want to miss that."

Actually, I really didn't want to miss it. Among the Mongolians working in our expedition were some really big, tough guys who, judging by their boasting, were champions in this special form of wrestling. But I realized that if I couldn't finish up my real assignment soon, I might have to miss the fun. What's the line from that old song my parents like to sing? "Summertime, and the living is easy?" Ha.

"And in the evening there'll be a big party," my dad chimed in, not noticing my gloomy expression. "Supposedly they pull all the jeeps and trucks into a circle, turn on the headlights, play Mongolian disco music on the radios, and go wild."

"Aided by plentiful quantities of fermented goat's milk," Dr. Longford added. "Not that young Zack here will have that, but there ought to be fruit soda brought all the way from Ulan Bator for the occasion."

Whoopee, I thought. Well, if we found the missing dinosaurs, the live ones, then maybe there would be something to celebrate.

Wow, I could even bring a date to the party—the beautiful and talented Cadet Vraj. Double ha.

At least the crazy picture of my parents' reaction when introduced to my date cheered me up. I certainly needed some cheering.

CHAPTER FIVE

The next morning, I woke before dawn and was too tense to go back to sleep. I dressed, crawled out of my tent, and watched the diamond-bright morning star slowly fade into sunrise. Soon piles of pink clouds rose into a baby-blue sky. They might have looked sappy in a painting, but here, it was spectacular. Swallows began swirling out of their cliffside nests, whistling and darting through the chill air—air that smelled like sage, mint, and wild onion. I would have felt perfectly at peace, if it weren't for this assignment.

I could hear a herd of goats coming nearer, every "baa" with a different tone. Some sounded like baby toys and some, like they'd swallowed a New Year's Eve noisemaker. I tried focusing my implant on them. I was definitely getting better at it, but they weren't talking about dinosaurs. Mostly it was stuff like, "Where's Mama?" "Better grass here." "I got to the top of the rock before you!"

Sighing, I pulled on my backpack and headed down to the cook tent. No one else was up yet except the cook. Thankfully she hadn't finished making the goat milk porridge yet so I got away with breakfasting on stale dough balls. I stuffed a bunch more in my pack for later.

Outside, Jargul and Segi were already waiting for me, my tan horse beside their brown ones. I didn't see our other partner, but she popped up once we were out of sight of the camp.

"Tried some of the night creatures," Vraj grumbled, "but the only ones like me they reported seeing were the two oafs who took the egg fossil and notebooks from the other camp. And that was several days ago, before they all . . . went missing."

I translated part of that for Jargul and Segi then said, "So, what do you suggest now?"

"Well," Jargul said, "since the message said they were somewhere high, let's head up high. You can try talking to the creatures that like heights."

I looked around and sighed. This area was full of high places. I pointed at the peak towering over our camp. "That looks about the highest."

"Don't even point at that one!" Segi whispered. "It's the most sacred. We haven't ever dared go near the top. But we could try its flanks."

This meant riding around the mountain's many spurs to get to the easiest side to climb. As we rode, the sun rose, but it was immediately hidden behind a rising purple wall of cloud. The wind was a lot stiffer than before, and it didn't feel like the day was going to get as hot.

We began a wide circle of the mountain, riding with Jargul and Segi well in the lead. Vraj trotted beside me, staying a little distance from my still slightly skittish horse. At one point, Vraj stopped to talk with a marmot. Then she bent down and gobbled the fellow up.

She must have noticed my horrified expression and trotted closer, still picking tufts of brown fur out of her teeth. "So?" she challenged. "This is hungry work."

"But you shouldn't really eat our informants, should you?"

She shrugged. "That one didn't have anything useful to say. Look, I really prefer my meat well roasted with a nice cream sauce. But this is a hardship assignment." She patted the small pack fastened around her middle. "The nutrition pills they give us just don't cut it."

We continued on, leaving me to wonder if—now that I could sort of talk to animals—I would have a harder time eating things like beef and pork. This alien agent stuff just might drive me to vegetarianism. I didn't think I could talk with carrots anyway. And I certainly didn't plan to try.

Eventually we turned into a narrow valley that took us partway up the back of the mountain. When it became too steep and rocky for the horses, we left them in a side valley with plenty of grass and took to the rocks. We met a few round, furry things, who claimed to have never seen anything like Vraj and certainly didn't want to now. Nothing happened until we got to a bare, rocky, and very windy plateau. Then Jargul pointed to the valley that was now far below us.

"Looks like we have a few minutes to find some shelter," he said in a worried tone.

I looked where he was pointing but didn't see anything worrisome. In fact, it was too hazy to see much at all. Then I realized the haziness was a yellow cloud, slowly moving toward us like a huge, lumbering animal.

"Sandstorm," he said. "Doesn't look too bad, but you never know."

Feeling very exposed on this open plateau, we scurried to the other side, where a tumble of rocks formed a semicircle. It looked like one of those old animal corrals we'd found on survey. Thank you, ancient people.

We'd just reached the sheltering rocks when the wind developed a voice, an angry, raspy voice, and suddenly the yellow cloud was upon us. Hunching behind the rocks with the others, I closed my eyes and pulled up my jacket hood. That didn't do much to keep out the gritty sand. It pelted against us like tiny bullets, scouring our skin and filling our ears with pain and noise.

The storm seemed to go on for ages. Then slowly the howling softened. Finally I raised my head and opened my eyes. The wave of sand had rolled past us, trailing a few angry twisters in its wake.

We looked at each other and laughed—even Vraj. Each of us looked like a figure carved from sand. We stood up as we brushed away and spit out the yellow grit. "I hope the horses are all right," I said.

"They're Mongolian horses," Segi said proudly. "They're used to this sort of thing.

They'll have taken cover and will probably go back home on their own."

"Well, I'm not used to it," I commented, offering my water bottle around. "That was some storm."

"It was just a little one," Jargul said. "Out on the desert, they can last for days. Often storms like that come before a rainstorm, so we'd better get moving."

We all looked up at the sky and saw that it was indeed piling with bruise-colored clouds. Jargul shook his head and added, "Looks like we've been sitting here too long."

I followed his pointing finger and saw a big black bird circling above us. "Are they dangerous?" I asked.

"Not if we're alive. It's a *tas*, a vulture. It eats dead things, and we were here so long, it's checking us out."

"Okay, let's get moving," I said with a shiver, and all of us began climbing the rocky slope that rose behind our shelter. Halfway up, the circling shadow of the tas swept over me.

It felt nearly as creepy as when Granny had read my fortune in the knucklebones. I refused to look up. The shadow moved on, rippling over the rocks.

Finally we reached a ledge, and I forced myself to look up. The tas was circling closer. "Go away," I called. "Can't you see we're alive and kicking?"

It just squawked and dropped closer. With awkward back pedaling of huge wings, it landed in front of us. This thing was enormous. I'd never seen such a big bird. It hopped clumsily toward us, as big as a man in a really ugly bird costume.

"Shoo, shoo!" Jargul and Segi cried, but it ignored them.

Instead it stopped in front of Vraj, gave her a beady stare and croaked in tas-talk, "If you'd kindly die, I'd eat you. If not, I've got a message for you."

"For me?" I couldn't miss the slight quaver in Vraj's voice. This bird was as big as she was and even meaner looking.

"You're the only thing around as ugly as the big lizard who gave me the message. Want to hear it?"

"Yes."

"What you give me for it?"

"I'll let you get away without eating you," Vraj snapped.

"No good. I can fly. You can't."

Hurriedly I fumbled in my pack, but all I found to offer was some fried dough balls. The tas just knocked them out of my hand.

"Got anything better?" I whispered back to Jargul. Quickly he gave me a slab of dried goat meat. In seconds, the tas snatched that away, barely leaving my fingers behind. It swallowed the meat whole.

It swallowed and gagged and finally got it down. "Not bad," it said, "but not dead long enough."

"Your message?" Vraj demanded.

"Right. 'Being held inside main mountain. Kiapa Kapa making demands Galactic Union mustn't meet. Free us.' That's it. I'm off."

"Wait!" Vraj cried as the creature stretched its huge wings. "Where were they when they gave you this message?"

"Didn't agree to lead you there. Just deliver message. Unless you plan to die now, I'm off."

CHAPTER SIX

"What a nasty bird," I said, as we watched the great black tas soar off into the sky.

"It probably hoped we'd die of fright," Vraj snarled, "except I wouldn't give it the satisfaction. However, it looks like your human friends just might. Better talk to them."

Jargul and Segi were indeed round-eyed and looked rather pale. "The bird just had a message for us about the . . . the spirits we're trying to find. Supposedly they're 'being held inside the main mountain.' Does that give you any sort of clue?"

Jargul lowered his eyes. "Granny was right. You are special. We've never seen anyone deal with a tas like that."

"But that clue doesn't make things easy," Segi added. "This mountain would probably be the *main* mountain. But it's so sacred, we've never explored it very far. There are stories, though, about a cave near the top where hermits used to live. That's the only 'inside' I can think of."

"So I guess we go to the top of the mountain," I said. The wind was picking up again, and it felt like Jargul's prediction of a rainstorm would come true.

Again we climbed. Before, when I'd been climbing rocks on the survey, I hadn't used the alien abilities Sorn had once shown me. When I do that, I kind of zone out and just climb without thinking. On the archaeological survey, I had to be constantly on the lookout for ancient stuff. Now all that mattered was getting to the top, so I went into climbing mode.

Even when a snake coiled back and hissed at me, I barely paused. A smattering of anger and fear floated to me from the snake, and I hissed the same thing back twice as strong. The surprised reptile shot off and disappeared into a rocky cleft. I kept climbing.

I was way ahead of the others. But as I stepped onto what was almost the final ledge, I realized I was not alone. A very, very large sheep was facing me. It looked like his huge, coiled horns could tip me off the ledge with ease. He snorted surprise, but not a whiff of fear.

When Vraj pulled herself up beside me, the mountain sheep just snorted contemptuously, "Another one of *them*."

"Who's *them*?" I snorted back.

"Them. The ridiculously big lizards."

"Where are they?" Vraj asked eagerly.

"Trapped inside," the mountain sheep answered with a toss of his hugely horned head. Then he trotted off, ignoring our pleas for more information.

From a slightly lower ledge, Jargul and Segi watched this interchange, and their awed expressions were almost embarrassing. I was beginning to wish that Vraj and I *did* have some kind of spiritual powers. Then maybe all these animals wouldn't be so ornery.

Again, I gave the two Mongolian kids an edited version of our conversation. "The big sheep said the . . . spirits we're looking for are trapped inside. So I guess we'd better keep looking for that cave."

There wasn't much farther up to go. The ledge we were on led like a ramp up to a boulder-strewn plateau. There certainly wasn't any sign of a cave. At one end of the plateau was a large tumble of rocks that probably counted as the mountain peak.

"So where's this cave?" Vraj grumbled. I asked Jargul, but he just shook his head.

"We've never been up here before. But the stories say that holy hermits lived here for years. So it couldn't have been just cracks between rocks."

Still, the rocks at the plateau edge were the only place to look, assuming this was the right mountain. I certainly wouldn't put much trust in directions given by either that nasty bird or that snotty sheep.

As we walked toward the rocks, the wind became heavy and wet, splatting us with large raindrops. At first, the smell of rain on the dry, dusty granite was soft and fresh. But the drops got faster and colder and hit with more force. Thunder suddenly rocked us with the sound of a giant dropping his toolbox. And almost at the same moment, the purple cloud above us lit up with lightning. We began running toward the rocks, which had almost disappeared behind the wind-lashed rain.

The rocks weren't much shelter, though. We scrambled about looking for some kind of overhang, until finally Segi cried that she'd found a narrow cleft we could just squeeze into. She, Jargul, and I managed, but Vraj almost got jammed in the entrance. I didn't know that dinosaurs didn't like rain, but this one apparently didn't. She yelled at us to squeeze farther back so she could fit. We tried, and suddenly Segi yelped and disappeared.

"There's a cave in here," her voice echoed from the darkness behind us. "And it's dry. Careful of the drop."

Jargul and I soon joined her and, finally, Vraj did as well, cursing in Tirgizian about worthless, rocky planets and scraping her lovely skin.

Ignoring her, I said to Segi, "Good work. I guess this must be your hermit cave. It isn't too sacred and forbidden for you to come in here?"

She shrugged apologetically. "Not when the other choice is drowning."

"Besides," Jargul added, "I'm sure if the spirit of the old hermit is still around, he'd make exceptions. We are trying to help other spirits, after all."

I felt a jab of guilt for having given them that line. But if there was one thing absolutely clear in my assignments, it's that humans are not to know that there are aliens around.

With the dark curtain of rain falling outside, we couldn't see much of this cave.

Then I remembered the flashlight in my pack and pulled it out. Vraj was also fumbling in her pack and pulled out a rod that glowed in a very alien-looking way. But then it could be seen as a spirit light too. I suppose people see what they expect.

The narrow cleft we'd crawled through led to a higher, wider channel in the rock. We followed it back until it opened into a room about the size of our cook tent, except that instead of canvas, the walls and ceiling were great slabs of stone. The soaking wind couldn't follow us there. For a while, we just huddled out of the storm, listening to thunder shake the mountaintop. I shared some fried dough balls from my pack. Vraj rejected these but took some of the dried meat Segi offered. Then we began exploring.

Vraj and I played our lights over the rock walls. The rocks were smooth, dark orange marked with lighter splotches. After staring at them a while, I suddenly realized these weren't splotches but drawings pecked into the surface of the rock. We'd seen drawings like this on our archaeological survey. These looked like pictures of goats with long, curving horns. They marched silently around the cave walls, occasionally joined by figures that looked like horses or big cats.

"Maybe a bunch of ancient hunters holed up here during storms and passed the time drawing goats," I suggested.

"Or they could have been offering goats to the spirit of the mountain," Segi said.

Jargul added, "Or maybe hunters were working magic, so they could catch more goats."

Vraj just growled, "Goats are not what we're looking for—though I wouldn't mind one for lunch right now." I did not translate that for the others.

She was right, though. If all this cave had to offer was ancient goat drawings, we were on the wrong track. "Let's look carefully to see if there's a passage leading somewhere else," I said in Mongolian.

We searched every crack with our lights. It was Jargul who noticed something important.

"Look how there are a lot of goats drawn on this rock wall, all marching to the left. And then there's a bunch more on that wall over there, also marching left. But there are no goats on the rock wall in between them."

He was right. The panel between was plain dark-orange rock.

Vraj snorted. "So the hunters got bored with drawing and not eating. I too have better things to do than hanging around this heap of rocks." With that, she kicked the middle panel of rock. It shook slightly.

"Was that thunder shaking the mountain," I asked, "or did you make that happen?"

"Hmmm," she said, examining the rock more closely. Then she kicked it again. It definitely moved a little, and a thread of rock dust dribbled to the floor. With a growl that sounded like a ninja warrior's, Vraj threw herself against the edge of the panel. The rock made a sharp grating sound, then it shifted inward.

"A door!" the rest of us cried at once, and we all joined in pushing.

Slowly the opening grew, letting out a wave of cold, dank, dead-smelling air. Finally, the gap was wide enough for Vraj. But instead of pushing herself through, she squatted down. With her light rod, she slowly examined the ground beyond the door.

"It doesn't look like this door has been opened for ages. The dust's undisturbed. The kidnappers certainly didn't bring any Tirgizians this way."

Discouraged, I nodded and looked at the door. If adult Tirgizians were much bigger than Vraj, they wouldn't have been able to fit through it anyway, much less the cleft we'd crawled through at first.

After I translated for Jargul and Segi, Jargul peered past Vraj and said, "But it does look like there's a passage beyond. You said the spirits you're looking for are being held inside the mountain? Maybe this could take us there."

I nodded. "You're right, but I'm not sure about the 'us' part. This could be dangerous.

Caves are dangerous anyway, and the...the bad spirits could be very powerful."

Segi smiled. "Which is why you need us to help you out. Our Granny has taught us a lot about spirits."

"Yeah, but these—" I began, but Vraj interrupted.

"Let them come. It's their planet's future we're dealing with here. I hate to admit it, but we might need some help."

That was some admission from her. And she could be right. So, one by one, we squeezed through the partly open doorway. Darkness oozed around us, seeming to suck at our breath and our light. This might still be Earth, but just then, the inside of this sacred Mongolian mountain seemed plenty alien to me.

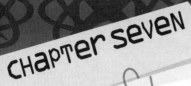

CHAPTER SEVEN

Lifting our lights, we looked around. "Ah, there are the other goats," Jargul said and pointed to the back of our door. On it, the missing goats continued in procession, and I realized that instead of a hinged door, this slab of rock pivoted. If we closed it by pushing it all the way around, the line of goats seen on the other side would be unbroken.

Segi said what we all felt. "Let's keep it open."

Walking a little farther into the dark, we could see that the ledge we were on ended at stairs, leading downward. Well, not stairs exactly, but scooped-out places in the rock.

We looked at each other and nodded. We had to see where they led.

Vraj went first, holding her glowing rod in front of her—then came Jargul and Segi. I took up the rear, holding my flashlight high so it could help light the way.

As we cautiously climbed down, I looked at the rock walls beside us and noticed that some had drawings on them. Not goats, but symbols I couldn't make out.

At a wide spot, we stopped in front of one, and Jargul said, "That's an inscription in old Mongolian script. See, it's written from top to bottom. I can't read it, though. They've stopped teaching it in schools."

Segi pointed to another inscription, written from side to side in sharp, swooping letters. "That's Tibetan, I think."

I nodded. "We saw some like it on the survey. Dr. Longford said it says something like 'O, jewel of the lotus.' I'm not sure what that means."

"It's a prayer," Segi explained. "That's one of the names of Buddha."

As we continued on, I was thinking that prayers were certainly something we could use about now. What awaited us at the bottom of these stairs might well be something we should not be dealing with. Not that we had much choice.

Ahead of us, the steps stopped at a broad ledge. We were surprised to see thin scraps of daylight, littered over the dusty floor.

"There's a little opening to the outside here," Jargul said, pointing to the rocky wall. "Phew, and there's a stink too."

He didn't have to tell us that. The lower we'd gone, the more it made me want to retch. It smelled like barnyards and dead animals. Vraj poked her light rod toward the little gray openings in the rock.

"There's a bunch of sticks out there. And something moving."

"Yes," a voice screeched. "Me!"

Twigs and pebbles burst aside as a face poked in at us. A familiar face. The tas.

"I wish you filthy creatures would stop ha-rassing my nest. First, that big scaly message-leaver, and now you. Either have the good manners to die right now or leave me alone!"

"Sorry," I screeched back, happy if my poor throat didn't have to talk tas much more. Then I turned to Vraj. "This must be where at least one of your Tirgizians came to deliver that message."

"Yes, but they must have been caught doing it." Her voice was more cracked than usual as she pointed her light to the rock floor. "Footprints . . . and blood."

Among the pebbles and churned-up dust were dark red splotches. I felt a moment's surprise that Tirgizian blood should be red. But I guess that made sense if their dinosaur ancestors and other Earth animals were related. Then I felt guilty, realizing that is wasn't the color that Vraj was concerned about. That blood could be from her parents.

"There's not much blood," I hurriedly pointed out. "The Tirgizian who left the message here probably got scratched in a scuffle when it was caught. See, there are more footprints on the stairs going down—but only a few drops of blood."

Vraj only grunted and continued down the stairs. We followed, and I couldn't help wonder what Jargul and Segi thought of spirits that could bleed.

The stairs were becoming broader and more regular, and on either side we glimpsed more inscriptions. Suddenly Vraj hissed and switched off her light. I did the same with mine. It took me a moment to realize that we weren't standing in total darkness. Our stairs were now winding down one wall of a cavern, and that big open space was lit by a faint light that seemed to be bleeding from somewhere out of sight.

Cautiously we crept down, straining to see in the misty grayness. What I finally saw made me catch my breath. I poked Segi, who was just ahead of me and pointed. Below us on the floor of the cavern was a huge figure. I hoped desperately it wasn't a hostile alien. Then I saw it was a statue. An enormous Buddha. It was carved into the rock wall opposite to the one we were climbing down.

We kept descending and soon were right across from the beautiful, serene, very peaceful face. The huge seated figure seemed to be quietly ignoring the disruption in its cave. And there definitely was disruption other than what we were causing.

From around a tall corner of rock, along with the faint light, came the sound of voices. Loud, very nonhuman voices. Vraj motioned a halt and strained to listen.

"The Kiapa Kapa are a mixed syndicate," she whispered. "Lots of species are involved. I think I hear Cloob, Porgatagi, and Gnairt."

I shivered. I had met Gnairt and didn't want to meet any more of them—or their friends, either.

Vraj began moving again. "We've got to get down there and see where they're holding the Tirgizians."

Trying to be as silent as ghosts, we continued down the stairs. Finally we reached the cavern floor. I glanced up at the big Buddha. Its face was lit with a calm half smile. I wished I could feel half as calm. I guess there's an advantage in being stone.

Vraj continued inching her way toward the corner of the rock wall. We followed, but she waved us back, snaking her head around the edge. Finally she pulled back and huddled us together. I tried to translate parts of what she said for the Mongols.

"The next cavern is even bigger than this one. There are about a half-dozen aliens walking around or working with devices on tables. I count four different species. The Tirgizian prisoners seem to be in a sort of cage of light that's set on a pile of rocks on the far side. It looks like the whole expedition is there—including my parents." She sank into a relieved silence for a moment, then continued. "I can't see any more without risking being seen."

"So what do we do now?" I asked, switching to Mongolian. "We're not exactly the best-equipped rescue team. I mean we don't even have any weapons with us."

"We have knives," Jargul offered. "We always carry them along with chopsticks."

Vraj snorted, then patted her pack and added with a fierce grin, "I have something more effective. Not that it's likely to be much use against the weapons the Kiapa Kapa will have."

"If you can talk with the spirits that are caged," Segi suggested, "they might have some suggestions."

Vraj grunted. I suspected she wanted to free the captives in some spectacular way all on her own and impress her parents. But obviously, she needed help. Without another word, she led us back into the shadows, skirting the stone Buddha to where we could inch along the far wall of the other cavern. Boulders and slabs along its base made it easier to stay hidden, but we had to be careful not to dislodge any loose, noisy stones.

The enemy aliens, though, were jabbering enough among themselves to cover our sounds.

I couldn't pick out much of what they said except occasional words like *transmission* and *financial potential*. And I had to fight the impulse to try to peer over the rocks and get a glimpse of the aliens who made up this Kiapa Kapa. But I figured that if I couldn't see them, they couldn't see me. And that's the way I wanted it.

As we got closer to our goal, I looked up and tried not to gasp.

On a flat rock outcrop sat a very large cage. Its sides seemed to be made from thin threads of violet light. Obviously those threads were strong, because they securely held creatures from a science-fiction nightmare inside. Eight very large dinosaurs were sitting, standing, or milling around. Instantly my mouth dried, and my palms got wet. I'd always loved monster movies. But I really did not want to be in the middle of this one.

Vraj crouched down and whispered, "We'll crawl up behind that cage, let

them know we're here, and," she added grudg-
ingly, "ask their advice."

Stealthily we made our way around the back
of the rock outcrop and then slithered up
toward the top. The cage seemed to keep any
noise the captives made locked inside it, but
the aliens in the cave sounded uncomfortably
near. We tried to be very quiet. As we neared
the top, we saw that the glowing violet threads
came down evenly like tent poles, but the
ground they met was not even. In spots, there
were little gaps.

Vraj pointed to these, then shrugged. I took
that to mean what I had realized too: the gaps
were much too small for the captive dinosaurs
to escape through. Then she pointed to me,
and I did not want to understand what *that*
meant. She pointed to me again, made little
walking motions with her claws, and then gave
me a shove.

Maintaining silence, I shook my head
violently. But I knew it was no use. Those
gaps were too small for Vraj too. Segi was the

smallest of us, but without an implant she wouldn't be much use, to say nothing of not wanting to put her in any more danger than she was in already.

Finally I nodded, slipped off my backpack, and crept toward the largest of the gaps. The glowing cage wall spanned a narrow crevasse, and by wriggling and shoving, I inched my way through. I popped my head up just in time to pull it down again as a large, scaly foot nearly stepped on me.

CHAPTER EIGHT

"Some vermin's creeping in here!" squawked a voice in Tirgizian.

Another creature shoved the speaker aside and peered down at me, where I crouched, shivering in the crevasse. Its teeth gleamed in the violet light. "No, it's one of the natives—a human."

"Greetings," I quavered, not venturing out. "I'm here with Vraj. We'd like to rescue you."

"About time," said another voice, and before I could yelp, a clawed hand pulled me into the cage. Soon I was crouched in the terrifying center of a circle of staring dinosaurs. I suppose if I had been thinking calmly, I would have seen that they were not quite like the ancient dinosaurs you see in books. Most were standing on two legs, and their hands had nimbler looking fingers. But they still looked fierce, even the ones with no sharp teeth.

In my little kid dinosaur phase, I'd learned the names of lots of dinosaurs. It sure looked like we had triceratops, duckbills, and tyrannosauruses right here. I was trying to get enough moisture in my mouth to talk when a couple of large velociraptors pushed their way toward me. Vraj's parents, I guessed.

"You must be the local agent here," one said. I couldn't tell if it was her mom or dad. It's easier to tell with mammals. But then the one talking said something very momlike. "Is Vraj all right? We're so worried about her."

"Yes. Vraj and a couple helpful natives are just outside." I glanced at the cage wall and realized you could not see out from the inside. "Is there anything you can tell us about why you are being held here or how this cage works, anything that could help us get you out?"

The duckbilled one grunted. "Fat chance these runts will have breaking us out of here. The Galactic Patrol needs to send a fleet."

The tyrannosaurus gave a ghastly, throaty laugh. "Don't be an idiot! That would totally violate Galactic Union policy. They'd sacrifice us before they'd lose a chance to bring this miserable planet into the Union."

"How can you say that about this planet?" wailed the triceratops. "It's our long lost ancestral home. Its safety is paramount!"

The tyrannosaurus growled, "Not more than—"

"Stop arguing!" the other velociraptor yelled, which was pretty brave considering that as big as it was, all the others were a whole lot bigger. "We've got to talk to this humanoid. You're the Galactic Union's local Agent, right? Zack Gaither?"

"Zack will do."

"All right, Zack, I'm Vraj's father. To answer your questions, the Kiapa Kapa is a syndicate of economic developers with strong criminal ties.

They are holding us ransom to force the Galactic Union to turn this planet over to them. They demand that the Union abandon its plans for Earth. Our investigation to determine that this planet was the birthplace of the Tirgizians is purely scientific. But that knowledge could also be exploited for enormous economic gain."

"How?" I asked.

"It's obvious," roared the T. rex. "Tourism. We Tirgizians have fantasized about our birth world for millennia. Most of our planet's population would jump at the chance to come here as tourists. And we are a very wealthy people. Think of the money that could be made by those running the tourist trade."

My imagination filled with images of dinosaurs in flowered shirts and sunglasses, trampling over the planet, snapping pictures, being crabby to the natives, and buying souvenirs. "Yeah, I see. And I don't think the native population would welcome that."

"Precisely," said Vraj's mom. "Not only would it scramble the local culture and economy, it would destroy any chance for a friendly entry of Earth into the Galactic Union."

I nodded. Camera-toting giant dinosaurs were probably not the first aliens that humans should be introduced to. But something left me puzzled. "What you just said would certainly be the position of the Galactic Patrol, but I got the impression from Vraj that you didn't exactly approve of her working for them."

The other velociraptor snapped, "That's because we wanted her to be a scientist like us—a nice safe profession, we thought—and not go gallivanting around the galaxy in the military." Then it leaned frighteningly close and whispered, "And if we all get out of this alive, we want Vraj to know how proud we are of her, just the same."

"Enough blather," announced the duckbill. "If these little creatures are going to get us out, they'll have to turn off the power in this cage. Opening the outer cave door would help too, while they're at it. Both impossible tasks, if you ask me."

With a swing of its meaty tail, the T. rex bumped the duckbill aside. "Listen then, boy. The controls for the cage and door and everything else in this hideout of theirs are in a booth on a ledge at the far end of the cavern. The problem is, of course, that it's guarded."

I looked up at this huge guy and couldn't help asking what I knew was a stupid question. "And there's no way you can break out using your size and strength? I mean, you *are* dinosaurs."

The T. rex laughed with the sound of falling rocks. "If strength were what it took, the Kiapa Kapa would be carrion. But the constraints on this cage are sonic. No amount of physical strength can dent them." To emphasize the point, its tail whacked against the glowing wall. It bulged out like a soap bubble, then snapped back.

But that turned out not to have been too bright a move. "Hey, what's going on in there?" a voice yelled from outside. Suddenly the wall became transparent from our side too. A tall creature with tentacles sticking out of its head like a giant sea plant stood outside. I dove behind the triceratops but not before the tentacled thing caught sight of me.

"Vermin! Native vermin in the cave! Kill it!" The creature raised what must have been a weapon, but I was already scrambling down the crevasse and out of there. Vraj, Jargul, and Segi were up and running when I snatched up my pack and joined them. We pelted over and around the rocks, heading back for the other cavern. Blasts of energy exploded behind us, filling the air with rock fragments and gouts of flame.

We charged into the semidarkness, darted behind the Buddha, and scrambled up the tumbled rocks beyond. Not daring to use our lights, we climbed by pure instinct. A few more shots erupted behind us but not as close as before. I was in the lead now and grabbed the others as they reached me, pushing them down behind a huge boulder.

Alien voices came from below. "What was it? One of those filthy things with horns? Or was it a stupid human?"

What must have been the tentacled thing answered. "I couldn't see clearly. But the modern humans don't know about this place."

"Then it was probably some cave creature that those miserable Tirgizians were trying to lure in to snack on. They don't appreciate our generous rations, I suppose." The laugh that followed was not a nice one.

"Still, we'd better keep a close lookout. We don't want any cave vermin fouling our equipment. Not with things going so well. We ought to be hearing the Galactic Union's response to our terms any time now."

The voices were receding, but I picked up a parting comment. "We'd better, or their precious Tirgizian scientists will become as extinct as their ancestors."

Vraj whispered, "This spot is too exposed if they decide to look for vermin again. There's a better hiding spot up farther."

"How can you tell?" I said, squinting into the darkness.

Vraj snorted. "I forgot, none of you have night vision worth anything. There's a side cavern at the top of this rockslide."

When I'd translated, Segi whimpered. "I don't think I can make it up there. I wrenched my ankle when we were running, and it's really starting to hurt."

"Why didn't you say anything?" Jargul asked.

"I was so scared, I hardly noticed it at the time."

"I can try to carry you," I offered.

"No, you can't," Vraj snorted. "You're so weak and clumsy you'll end up hurt like her. I'll carry her."

With that, the young dinosaur scooped up Segi and started clambering up the rock-strewn slope. More blindly, Jargul and I followed.

When we'd found our way to the side cave Vraj had seen, she whistled us to the back of the cave and turned on her glow rod to a low setting. A faint mist of light showed a tall cleft in the rocky mountain. One wall shielded us from the cavern below. Boulders the size of small cars laid scattered about.

"It's safe to talk here," Vraj said.

"But it's plenty smelly," I commented.

"I wouldn't know. I'm not afflicted with your primitive, overdeveloped sense of smell."

It did stink like rotten eggs, but I tried to ignore it as I told them what I'd learned from the captive Tirgizians.

When I'd finished, Vraj asked, "And my parents—and the others of course—were they all right? They hadn't been hurt?"

"They looked fine to me," I assured her, though the idea that large, toothy dinosaurs could look fine was a stretch for me.

Jargul summed things up. "So all we have to do is get to that control place, somehow let the captives out of the cage, and open the big door to the outside."

"Right," I said. That's all we had to do. Right. "Vraj, what kind of weapon do you have in that pack?"

"Standard Galactic-Agent issue. No good at all against sonic constraints."

"Well, maybe we could use it to create enough of a diversion to get to their control room and do something there. It's way on the other side of that cavern, though. It'd have to be some big diversion."

Vraj snorted. "May I point out that the Kiapa Kapa is never without a great many weapons themselves? But still, I should creep down there again and get a better look. At least they don't realize that a rescue party is at hand, despite you clumsily letting yourself be seen."

She ended with a bitter laugh that kept me from objecting. She was partly right. It was not my fault I'd been seen, but we sure weren't much of a rescue party.

"I'll go with you," I said instead.

"You will not. We don't need anyone else laming themselves in the dark. Stay here and fix that girl's ankle while I check things out. I'm off!"

With only a slight swish and clatter, my fellow agent vanished, leaving the three of us alone in the stinky dark under a huge mountain in the middle of Mongolia. This was definitely not the sort of pleasant summer vacation I could brag about to my schoolmates. Of course, if I didn't live through it, I wouldn't have to worry about that.

CHAPTER NINE

Vraj had taken her glow rod with her, but I switched on my flashlight and sat beside Segi. "Guess we'd better take a look at that ankle."

"I'm sorry I was so clumsy," she said as she rolled down her sock.

"No, I'm sorry I got you into this. Oh, that looks nasty."

Her ankle was already purple and swollen like a sausage. Vraj had told me to "fix that girl's ankle" when she left, as if that was something I could do. Of course, I should be able to. Some of the computer lessons from the Galactic Union had been about focusing energies into healing. But I'd never tried it on anyone but myself so far, and that had only been to heal minor cuts and scratches. I remembered how Sorn had used it on my cousin after the Gnairt attacked us. It had seemed so easy then. But now . . .

And of course, I didn't want to let them know I had any special alien abilities. So I'd have to change my approach. "Well, actually, it looks like it will go down pretty quickly by itself. Maybe I could massage it a little to hurry it along. That's . . . eh . . . what they suggested in my first aid class."

I put my hands on her ankle, closed my eyes, and tried to remember the lessons—the real ones. Focus my energies. Visualize the injuries. Visualize how I wanted them to change. My mind sunk into images of blood vessels, muscles, tendons, and discolored skin. I only came out of it when Jargul, sitting beside me, gasped.

Dizzily, I opened my eyes. The ankle under my hands looked like a normal ankle. I felt a flush of surprise and pleasure but quickly tried to hide it. "See, it's gotten better already. They do that sometimes."

Jargul just shook his head. "You're good. When Granny does healings, she uses incense and incantations and special oils."

Segi smiled. "She said we'd be in good hands with Zack."

I blushed, and then a wave of guilt just about choked me. I couldn't keep up with this game, not when I was endangering their lives.

"Segi, Jargul. Now that the ankle's better, I want you to go up those stairs we came down, walk out the cave door, find the horses, and go home. This business here is getting much too dangerous."

Jargul looked at Segi, then answered. "We can't. These are our mountains and our spirits. What affects them, affects us."

I could have screamed over the mess I'd created. "Look, you guys. I've got a confession to make. About those spirits. They're not really—"

Jargul held up his hand. "We know."

"What? You do?"

He smiled. "Well, we may not know all the things that you do. But we aren't living in the old times. We read. Sometimes we live in town. We watch television. This *is* the twenty-first century."

Segi nodded. "But just because that dragon and the others . . . and you, aren't like in the old stories, it doesn't mean you're not spirits in your own way. Some of you are good, some are bad, and which of you wins will make a difference in this place. So we've got to stay and help."

I stuttered a bit then finally came out with, "But you don't understand."

"We understand all we need to," Jargul interrupted.

"And I understand that my ankle's all better," Segi said as she jumped up and hugged me. "Now I just wish our dragon would come back so we can get going."

I laughed, trying to cover my embarrassment, I guess. "Right. This sure is a stinky place to have to wait for someone. What makes it smell so bad?"

Segi giggled. "That's easy. Bats."

"Bats?" I cried, looking nervously around. She grabbed my flashlight and shone it on the cave ceiling. It looked like the rock there was covered with dried leaves. Then one fluttered a wing. Bats. Hundreds of them. Thousands. I shivered.

Segi shown the light on the cave floor not far from where we sat. "Bat droppings, see. They sleep here in the day, then clouds of them fly out of the mountain at night. That's hundreds of years of bat droppings you smell."

"Gross. And creepy. Bats creep me out."

"Really?" Jargul said. "In Mongolia bats are bringers of good luck. That isn't so in America?"

"No, bats are creepy, evil things that hang out with vampires." Then I remembered the bat pendants I'd seen in the Ulan Bator gift shops. I'd thought they were for the international Goth tourists. "Well, if bats are good luck here, we ought to be majorly lucky about now."

The other two laughed, then silenced themselves as we heard something below us on the slope. I switched off my light, but in moments, Vraj's light replaced it.

"Okay, I've spied things out, but it doesn't look good. I've spotted the control booth and what must be the door to the outside, but they're both way across the cavern and well guarded. If we could just release the prisoners, they could jump the Kiapa Kapa, and someone could probably get to the controls and open the outside door. That doesn't seem to have any sonic controls. But my personal weapon is useless against sonic. I understand, Zack, that you have certain abilities too, but I don't think they'd work on sonic."

I shook my head. True, I did have certain abilities as she said. The mental powers I'd accidentally discovered could do a lot of damage. In my lessons, I'd been trying to learn how to use and control them so they didn't damage me as well. But it all had to do with light and molecules, not sound.

"So what do we do?" I said and flinched as something darted past me in the air. "Ugh. I'm still not too fond of bats."

"It must be almost evening," Segi said. "They're waking up and getting ready to fly out and look for insects. There must be an opening further up this slope."

Evening, I thought. I'd already missed the wrestling my parents had wanted me to see, and now I'd miss the famous Disco-in-the-Desert party too. If I lived through this, I'd have to come up with some good excuses.

Another little, furry body zipped past us with a high-pitched squeak.

"Bats!" I cried, suddenly standing up.

"I believe we have already established that," Vraj said with a sneer.

"No! I mean, bats are sonic. They use sonar to navigate. Maybe if enough of them flew into the big cavern, they'd disrupt the sonic constraints."

Thoughtfully, Vraj scratched her reptilian head. "Yes, but until the main door's open, there's no way out down there. Segi just said they'll exit the mountain farther up."

"So, we've got to persuade them to change their little minds."

They all looked at me quizzically. I grinned. "It's talk-to-the-animals time!"

Already more of the little flying rodents were dropping off the ceiling and fluttering around like autumn leaves. Over their fluttering, I called to the other three, "I don't know how bright they are. We could ask for their help, but I'm not sure they'd see much in it for them. But maybe we can get them angry and then convince them that their enemy is down below in the big cavern. What do you think?" The two Mongolians nodded, but Vraj didn't answer.

I cleared my throat. "Okay. Jargul, you and Segi throw rocks up at them. Vraj, you and I need to do some powerful bat-talk." I sat on a rock, but she didn't move. "Okay?"

She shrugged. "A stupid-sounding idea. But it's all we've got."

Jargul and Segi picked up rocks from the cave floor and hurled them up at the hanging curtain of bats. In angry clumps, the creatures dropped free and began fluttering overhead. More rocks, and soon the whole massive colony was swirling and darting above us. I crouched down and squeaked for all I was worth. "Enemy way below in big cave. Attacking you. Must attack them. Yell at them, dive at them. Attack, attack, attack!"

Vraj seemed to be doing the same, but it was hard to hear anything over the flapping and enraged squeaking of the bats. I tried to fight down my horror-movie-induced terror of bats. They were swirling around me like a fluttery black cloud. I hoped they were getting the idea that *we* were not the enemy. Then, as if guided by remote control, they clumped into a huge cloud and swept down the slope. We jumped up and watched them fly over the Buddha statue and into the large lit cavern beyond.

"Hurry!" Vraj yelled. "We've got to get down there!

Like mountain goats, we four all hopped over the rocks and followed the squadron of bats. When we reached the edge of the big cave, their attack was obviously having its effect. The Kiapa Kapa aliens were dodging and ducking and shooting their energy weapons with little results. Bats are awfully quick.

I looked anxiously at the cage holding the Tirgizians. The raging sonic interference seemed to be doing something. The cage's glowing bars were turning from violet to throbbing purple. Suddenly with an electric pop and sizzle, they vanished. The trapped dinosaurs didn't take long to break free.

This was our chance at the main controls, I thought, as the Tirgizians bounded out of their cage and eagerly joined the battle. But the control booth was on the far side of the cavern, and the battleground lay between.

A bloated humanoid Gnairt was trying to fend bats off with a chair. An alien that looked like a tower of pebbles was hopping frantically away from an infuriated tyrannosaurus.

I glimpsed Jargul hurling rocks at something purple and hairy, and Vraj was gleefully using her own energy weapon. Something she hit with its glowing beam exploded like a fiery balloon, splattering green goo everywhere.

Trying to skirt the battle, I charged toward the control booth near the far wall. Angry bats were everywhere. I ducked, threw my arms over my head, and tried to plow through them. Suddenly I tripped over something. As I rolled across the cave floor, I dizzily looked back. A fat, bald Gnairt was glaring at me. He snatched up a weapon and aimed it my way.

I'd been practicing mental weaponry in our backyard, but all that came to me then was defense. I threw out a ragged energy shield just in time to deflect his deadly fire. The beam bounced off and smashed into the cave wall, sending up a geyser of rock and dust. But its force sent me bouncing backward. I landed on something that felt like a porcupine and squealed like a pig. With scaly hands, it tried to grab me as I leaped up. Suddenly it was catapulted into the air by a rooting triceratops, the same triceratops that had just stomped on the Gnairt.

I yelled a thank you over my shoulder as I raced on. In several bounds, I reached the top of the broad rock ledge and stumbled into the shiny metal booth. Once inside though, the controls dumbfounded me. There were so many buttons, gauges, and levers. Screens showed strange symbols, and lights glowed or flashed. How was I to open the outside door?

Holding my breath, I reached out a hand and pressed a button. Instantly the tall, blank cave wall outside the booth blossomed into a giant moving picture of dinosaurs, ancient ones, walking and fighting in a swampy forest. Great. It looked like the Kiapa Kapa had made a spectacular holographic movie about past Earth to thrill their hoped-for tourists. Terrific, but that didn't help this jail break.

I started to press another button, then realized I could as likely blow myself up as open the outer door. *So, okay, Alien Agent,* I told myself. *Do* something *alien!*

Closing my eyes, I spread my hands toward the controls and tried to remember those alien computer lessons. All I'd used them for at home was exploding rocks and mentally dismantling a clock. But Vraj and her weapon were somewhere fighting in the cavern, and I was all the weapon we had in this control booth.

I tried to send my mind into the lit-up panel and feel around. A bunch of confusing alien stuff—symbols, circuits, and computer synapses. I couldn't figure it out. I'm no alien engineer. But I didn't have time to do things nicely anyway. Just destroy it!

Frantically I channeled power from one set of mysterious devices into another—depleting one, overloading the other. Soon the control panel was glowing, and then smoking. Deep into the channels of power now, I happily continued shunting and pressuring. Suddenly claws sank into my shoulder and yanked me back, dragging me like a sack down the rocks.

Above me, the control booth erupted with the sound, light, and heat of a volcano.

CHAPTER TEN

I don't think I totally passed out. The pain of claws in my shoulder never left me. Something picked me up and bounded behind a boulder as a shower of rocks, ash, and hot bits of metal poured down on us. The sounds of explosion mixed with grating rock. Then came roaring, snarling, and finally thundering feet.

As it all died down, I looked at the creature crouched beside me. "Hurry up if you want to thank me," Vraj said dryly. "My fellow Tirgizians have barreled out of here, and I've got to stick with them."

"Thank you?" I said, rubbing my throbbing shoulder. Fuzzily I remembered being mentally locked into the ready-to-explode controls. "Right. Thanks."

"Anytime, Agent Zack. Bye." With that, Vraj leaped up like a kangaroo and bounded toward the wall of the cave. Only now there was a large open door in the cliff. The last of the fleeing dinosaurs, Kiapa Kapa, and bats were pouring out of it.

I staggered to my feet and looked around. Jargul and Segi were standing in the middle of the cavern floor. They saw me and waved frantically.

"Hurry!" Jargul yelled. "That explosion loosened some rock. It's starting an avalanche!"

I didn't waste time looking. It sounded like half the cave wall behind me was coming down. Forgetting my cuts and bruises, I sprinted to the others and the open cave door. We'd just reached it when huge slabs of rock broke free and crashed down on the blasted remains of the control booth. Other rocks rained down until the original floor of the cavern was completely buried.

Coughing and half blinded by the dust, we stumbled through the door. Cool night air surrounded us. We gulped at it thirstily. Then the three of us stumbled farther from the cave before sinking to the ground, shaking and laughing with relief.

Slowly our laughter died, replaced by a new very odd sound. Through the night came the distant, tinny sound of music. Disco music. I looked up. Some distance away, I could see flashing lights. They didn't look like spaceship lights. They looked like the headlights on trucks. Disco in the desert! All those steps inside the mountain must have taken us way down to its base.

Jumping to our feet, we hurried toward the lights and music. In the circle of trucks, we saw a bunch of huddled humans. Then two popped up and ran toward us.

"Zack!" my mom called, engulfing me in a hug. "There you are! Are you all right? We were so worried."

"Did you see all that?" My dad yelled as he hugged me next. "What on Earth happened?"

There was certainly no way I could answer that. "Eh . . . yeah. What do you think happened?"

Dad laughed. "Well, one thing that obviously happened was that we all drank too much of that fermented goats' milk. I swear I saw the whole mountainside light up with a picture of dinosaurs walking through ancient swamps." He shook his head and laughed again. I suddenly realized that the holographic tourist film must have been projected on the outside of the mountain as well as inside.

Still chuckling, my dad continued the story. "And then there was a big explosion—an avalanche, I guess—and it looked like real dinosaurs were galloping over there. Must have been a goat herd, but it sure spooked us."

Several others were crowding around us now, but they parted as a little bow-legged lady in an orange robe hobbled up. Segi and Jargul cried joyfully and hurried forward to hug her.

"Granny came this afternoon to bless the wrestling," Mom said. "We were surprised she decided to stay for the party, but she seemed to like the music."

"If I didn't know she was such a sweet old lady," my dad said, "I'd suspect she'd slipped some hallucinogenic herbs in the drink. Those dinosaurs sure looked real."

When Jargul roughly translated for her what my dad said, Granny laughed.

"The spirits were quite strong enough without my help," she said, with a wink for her grandchildren and me.

When that was translated into English, the others laughed at the words. I laughed at the meaning.

Thankfully, no one pressed us for more details. Segi, Jargul, and I were all given big bowls of leftover barbecued goat. Then Granny and her grandchildren rode off, and I walked with my parents and the others back to camp. My sleeping bag never felt so good.

The next morning, I slept late. By the time I crawled out of my tent, I had my story all figured out.

But it turned out that some of the expedition members, including my parents, whose fermented goat milk hangovers weren't too bad, had already gone to explore the now-open cave. Uncertainly, I went to join them. Peering in the opening, I saw the entire cave floor piled deep with rocky rubble. I hoped any sign of aliens was thoroughly buried.

The front cavern where the aliens had been was now empty, but I heard happy, excited voices from the cavern beyond. Picking my way across to it, I saw people shining flashlights on the giant Buddha and the inscriptions on the wall.

Seeing me, my parents and Dr. Longford hurried over. "Isn't this wonderful?" my mom cried.

"It's fantastic! It's the find of the season!" Dr. Longford exclaimed.

I smiled. The story I'd concocted just might work. "Yes, that's why we were so late yesterday. Jargul, Segi, and I were exploring the mountain. We found a cave and a hidden doorway up at the top. The stairs led down here, and we saw the statue. But maybe all the thunder yesterday shook the mountain so much that it set off an avalanche."

"You are very lucky you weren't crushed," Mom said, hugging me again.

Longford nodded. "And we are lucky the avalanche burst open the side of the caves. We have so much wonderful work to do here!"

After a while, I left them, all happily exploring. I had some exploring of my own to do, but I didn't know where to begin. Last night a whole flock of aliens had burst out of that mountain and scattered over the Mongolian desert. Where were they now?

I set out into the desert, heading toward a distant rocky knoll, the highest point in the barren plain. Maybe from there I could see something, maybe footprints, maybe... I don't know what.

I was certainly surprised at what I did see.

Below me in a little dry valley, two people were sitting talking. One with a shaved head and orange robe—Granny. The other was a woman with Western clothes and very white hair. Bewildered, I stumbled down toward them. "Sorn?"

They both looked up and smiled. "Well, Zack, join us," Agent Sorn said in Mongolian. "I've been having the most enlightening talk with this wise woman here."

Was Sorn trying to pass herself off as a wandering tourist? I must have looked confused.

Granny grinned and patted a seat on the rock beside her. "Don't be troubled, boy. This is my land, and I understand a great deal about it. About its spirits, the ones that walk here now, and the ones that walked here long, long ago. The land is always happy to see its own return, no matter how far they must travel."

I looked questioningly at Sorn. She smiled. "This is a woman who knows and can keep many secrets."

Laughing, Granny stood up. "And so can my grandchildren, twenty-first century though they may be. You are always welcome in our yurts, Zack, no matter what world you call home."

With that, she hobbled off toward her horse waiting nearby. In moments, she was trotting over the grassland toward distant yurts.

I turned my gaze to Sorn. "Remarkable woman," she said. "This planet certainly produces some amazing creatures. It has for millions of years, it seems."

"So what happened? Where are the Tirgizians? The Kiapa Kapa? And why are you here?"

Agent Sorn laughed. "First me. As soon as the Kiapa Kapa transmitted their demands to the Galactic Union, we dispatched a squadron. But we didn't dare intervene until we heard from you or Vraj, or had some better inkling of how things stood. We were monitoring the site as best we could, however. When all of their equipment exploded—largely your doing, I understand—we slipped down here."

"Well, Vraj and the two Mongolian kids did a lot too. But then what happened?"

"We eventually found and rounded up everybody. This Kiapa Kapa Syndicate is headed for jail, and the Tirgizian scientists are headed back home with a scientific triumph. They promise to wait until Earth is ready, however, before they come again."

"And Vraj?"

"She'll be heading back to the Academy with high honors. Seldom has a Cadet Agent performed so well on assignment."

"I'm glad. This Agent career sure means a lot to her. Oh, I forgot. Her parents wanted me to deliver a message to her."

Sorn laughed. "I think they delivered it themselves. They really are quite proud of her—just as I am proud of you."

We sat in silence awhile, looking over the rolling landscape, which after yesterday's rain had suddenly turned more green than brown.

Sorn sighed and looked at me. "If your life goes on like this much longer, we may have to tell your parents about you too. Leading a double life can be hard."

For a moment my stomach clenched. Did I really want my parents to know I was an Alien Agent? I'd gone through a lot of change in this last year. Did I want more?

Slowly I answered. "Yes, it's hard, but I don't know if they . . . if I . . . if *we* are quite ready for that just yet. The same way Earth isn't quite ready for dinosaur tourists."

Sorn chuckled and stood up. "Well said. So I guess I must leave you now, free to enjoy a real vacation here at the ends of the Earth, as you called it."

She walked to a large rock and pulled from behind it what looked like a streamlined silvery motorcycle. It hummed into life as she mounted it. Then with a wave she sped away, soon disappearing into the distance. My gaze shifted from the thin trail of dust behind her to the great arching bowl of blue sky.

The ends of the Earth. The kids back at school certainly will be impressed. Yurts, horseback riding, dinosaur fossils. I'll just keep some of the details to myself.

Laughing, I stood up. The problem with being a *secret* agent, of course, is the secret part. But that was okay for now. Alien or not, Earth was home—at whatever end.

alien encounter

[BOOK #4 OF THE
alien agent
series]

pamela F. Service
illustrated by mike gorman

TOP SECRET
from
ALIEN ENCOUNTER

VOICE RECOGNITION CONFIRIMED

BEGIN TRANSMISSION....

I had just returned home from a secret assignment for the Galactic Union. It finally looked like the rest of my summer could be a normal human-kid-type summer.

Wrong.

I was in the kitchen rummaging in the fridge for an afternoon snack. Then my mom came in with the mail. She handed me a fat envelope. I didn't recognize the return address. But when I opened it, I discovered that I had won an essay contest. My essay, "What I'd Do If I Met a Real Alien," had won an all-expenses-paid trip. One parent and I would travel to Roswell, New Mexico, for their annual UFO festival.

The problem was that I had never entered any contest.

But I knew enough to recognize this was the Galactic Union messing with my life again. So I acted happy in front of my mom. Then I escaped upstairs to my room. I dropped into the swivel desk chair. Taking a deep breath, I switched on my computer.

Sure enough, there was an incoming message from my boss, Agent Sorn. Locking my bedroom door, I made the coded entry. Sorn's smiling purple face popped up on my screen. She looked kind of apologetic.

"Zack, you should have your packet now. I'm sure you'd like a little explanation."

I tried not to look as annoyed as I felt. So much for my hopes of a normal human summer. Still, my curiosity stirred a little. Sorn raked long fingers through her hair. It stood up like a polar porcupine's. "Have you ever heard of the so-called flying saucer crash in Roswell, New Mexico, back in 1947?"

I thought a moment. "Yeah, I think I saw a TV program about it once." I didn't remember much. That was before I had any personal interest in aliens, after all. "But didn't it turn out to be a hoax or something?"

"Your government would like you to believe that. They put out several cover-up stories. Said it was really a weather balloon and such. But, no, it was real. A real alien ship did crash."

"Whose?" I knew enough by then to realize there were nearly as many types of aliens as stars in the sky.

"Nythians. The Galactic Union had placed Earth off

limits. They warned interstellar travelers to stay away
No one was to interfere before Earth's civilization had
reached a higher level of technology and stability. Bu
we didn't have enough personnel to really enforce it. The
Nythians are kind and peaceful but very private. They're
not known for joining groups or obeying rules. They're
also a very curious people. They'd become interested in
Earth and concerned about it getting nuclear weapons. A
number of Nythian ships visited Earth in the 1940s and
1950s. Some were seen, but most humans didn't take the
sightings seriously.

The big problem came in July of 1947. One Nythian
ship was damaged in an electrical storm. It crashed near
Roswell. Several civilians found the crash site first, and
word leaked out. But soon the U.S. military whisked
away the wreckage and the bodies of the crew. Then they
tried to hush things up."

I was stunned. "So the government does know about
the existence of aliens!"

"Actually, only a small group knew the truth. Other
people in the government believed the denials. Evidence

would have been slim because Nythian bodies turn to dust shortly after death. A crashed ship is programmed to self-destruct automatically. Crew members have only a short time to cancel that."

This was interesting, but I didn't see how I fit in. "So what's the problem? That was long ago. What does it matter now?"

Sorn gave a tired little laugh. "We didn't think there was a problem until recently. Oh, some humans latched on to the story of a UFO crash and short, bug-eyed aliens. Books and magazines about UFOs popped up. Roswell became the center for UFO believers and hokey alien souvenirs. They even hold an annual UFO festival there. Quite harmless really."

Sorn was becoming annoyingly dramatic, stretching out the story like this. "So what changed?"

She sighed. "Recently we learned about a Nythian child named Tu, the son of one of that ship's crew. He has—what's the Earth phrase?—yes, developed 'a bee in his bonnet.' He believes his father somehow survived the crash and is still on Earth. It seems this kid has stolen a ship. He's headed toward Earth. According to his worried mother, his idea is to go to Roswell while they are having their festival. He hopes to learn if there were any survivors and if his father might be one of them."

Something wasn't making sense to me. "Sorn, that was more than sixty years ago. The dad wouldn't be young anymore. And even if he survived the crash, he probably wouldn't be alive now."

Sorn shook her head. "We're not talking about humans here, Zack. Nythians mature very slowly. They have very long lives. The real danger is that the young Nythian will get himself caught. Nythians tend to be rather naive and trusting. If the U.S. government or UFO enthusiasts get their hands on a real space alien, who knows what would happen? It could certainly destroy the Galactic Union's plans. We hope for a gradual introduction to the idea that other planets are inhabited."

I was beginning to get the drift of this. "So my job is . . . what? Find this kid and tell him to go home?"

She smiled. Her amethyst-colored eyes actually twinkled. Her species can do that. "That's right. You've become quite a capable agent, Zack, even though your training isn't complete. You're clever and resourceful. I'm sure you'll be able to carry this out. And whichever parent you choose to go with you won't even catch on."

I just grunted.

Sorn looked concerned. "I do hate dumping all these tasks on you. But this is very important, Zack. So much depends on you. You don't mind too much, do you?"

I managed to smile and shake my head.

"Good." She sounded relieved. "And anyway, this is really a simple assignment. And it also gives you a fun little vacation."

Sorn is a nice person. The Galactic Union seems to be a fine outfit with a mission I'm proud to be part of. But I have got to learn not to buy statements like that.

Simple and fun? Yeah, right.

END TRANSMISSION

about the author

Pamela F. Service has authored more than 20 books in the science fiction, fantasy, and nonfiction genres. After working as a history museum curator for many years in Indiana, she became the director of a museum in Eureka, California, where she lives with her husband and cats. She is also active in community theater, politics, and beach combing.